ISBN: 978-1-911171-38-6
Order from www.flyingeyebooks.com

Mauro Gatti

PING vs PONG

Flying Eye Books
London | New York

Once, not too long ago, two special edamame beans were born on the very same day.

These beans shared a dream to become the greatest table tennis players in the world.

So they trained all day...

...and all night...

...and over time,

they beat
EVERYBODY!

WINNING IS FU

Their dream had come true.

They were the best table tennis players in the world.

But that wasn't enough! The world wanted
to know which player was the very best of all.

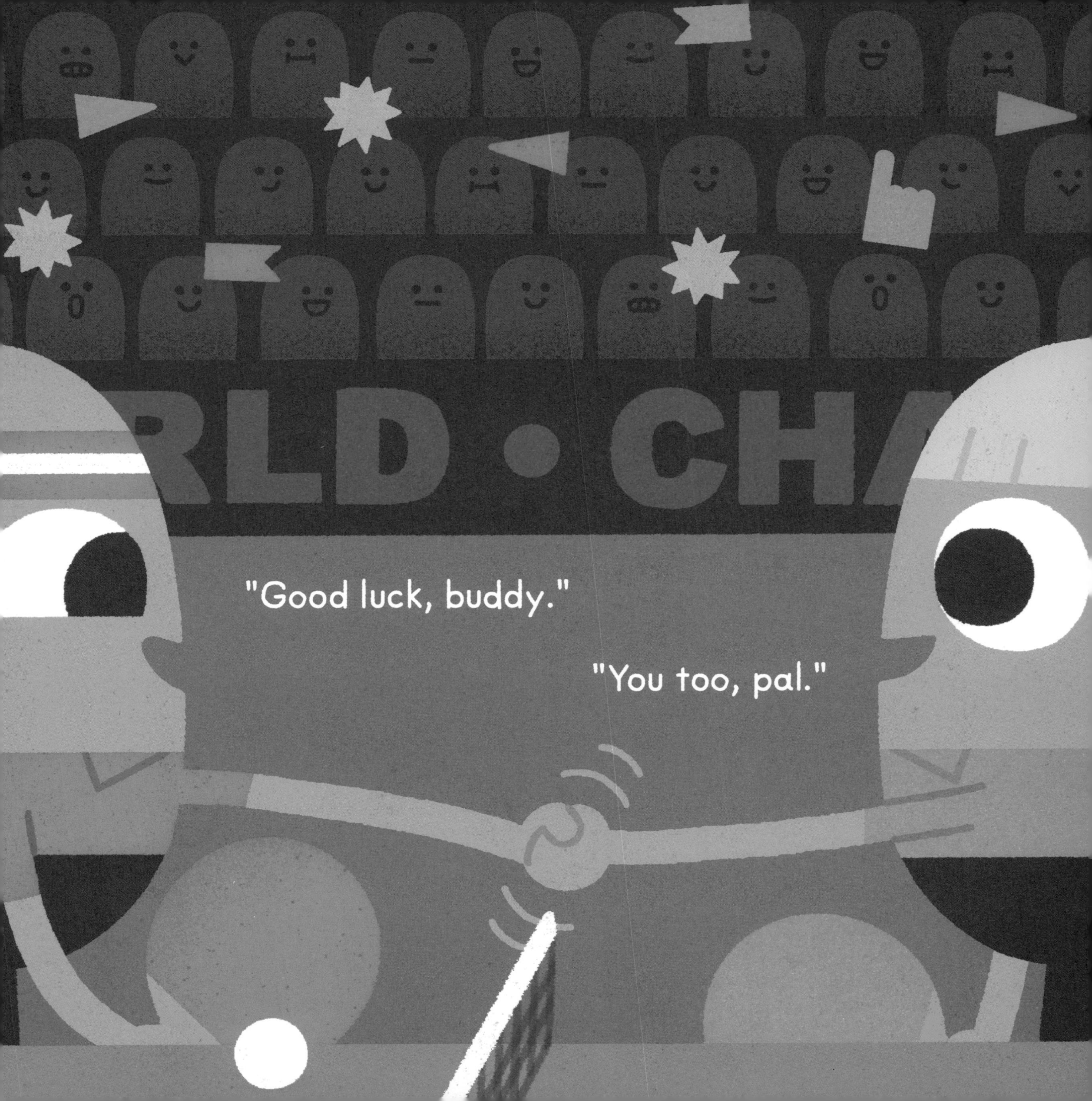

"Good luck, buddy."

"You too, pal."

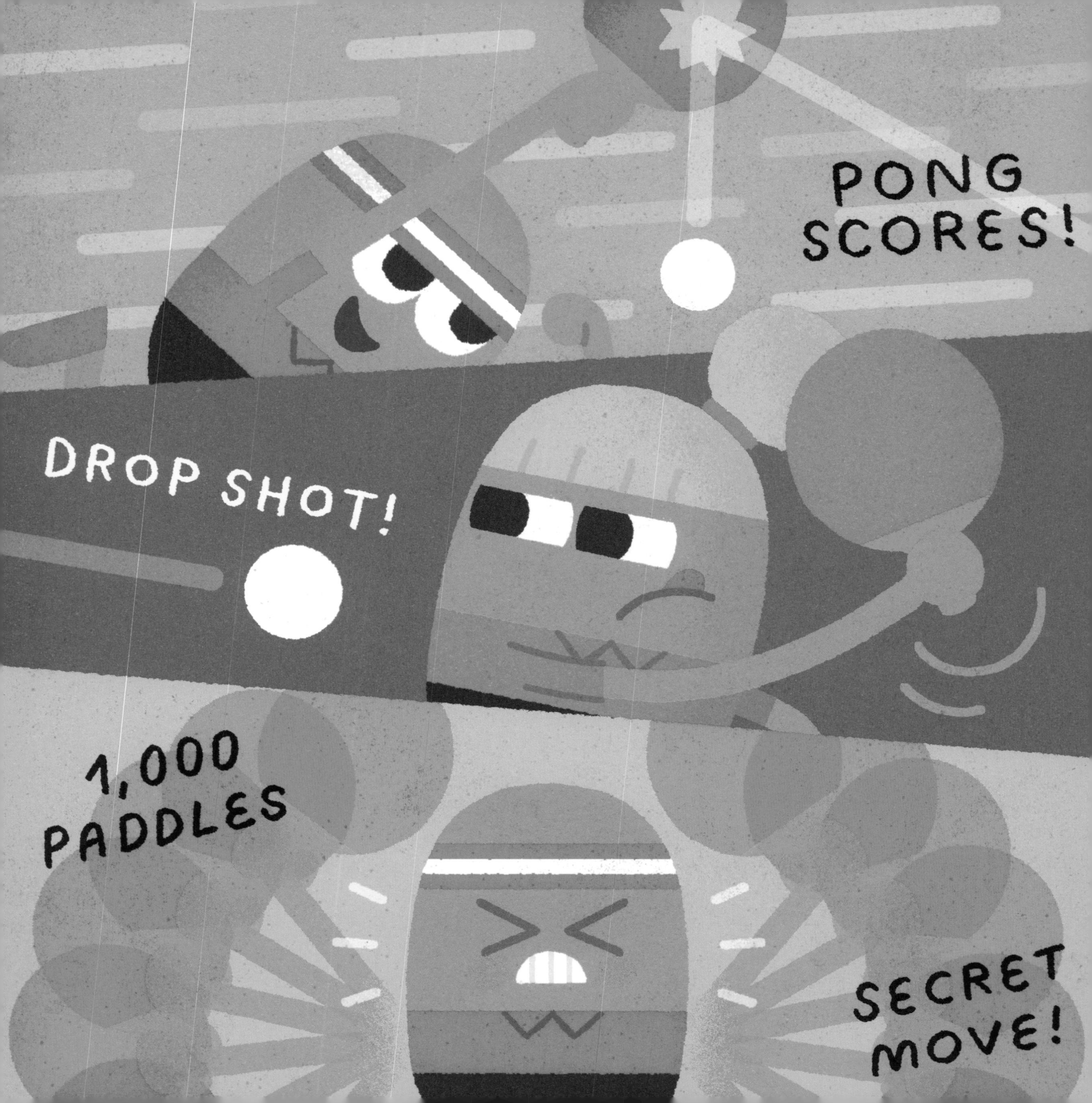
PONG SCORES!
DROP SHOT!
1,000 PADDLES
SECRET MOVE!

Their scores were tied.

PING 10

PONG 10

It was time for the game point.

Suddenly, something terrifying dawned on Ping and Pong. For the first time ever, only one of them would be the winner.

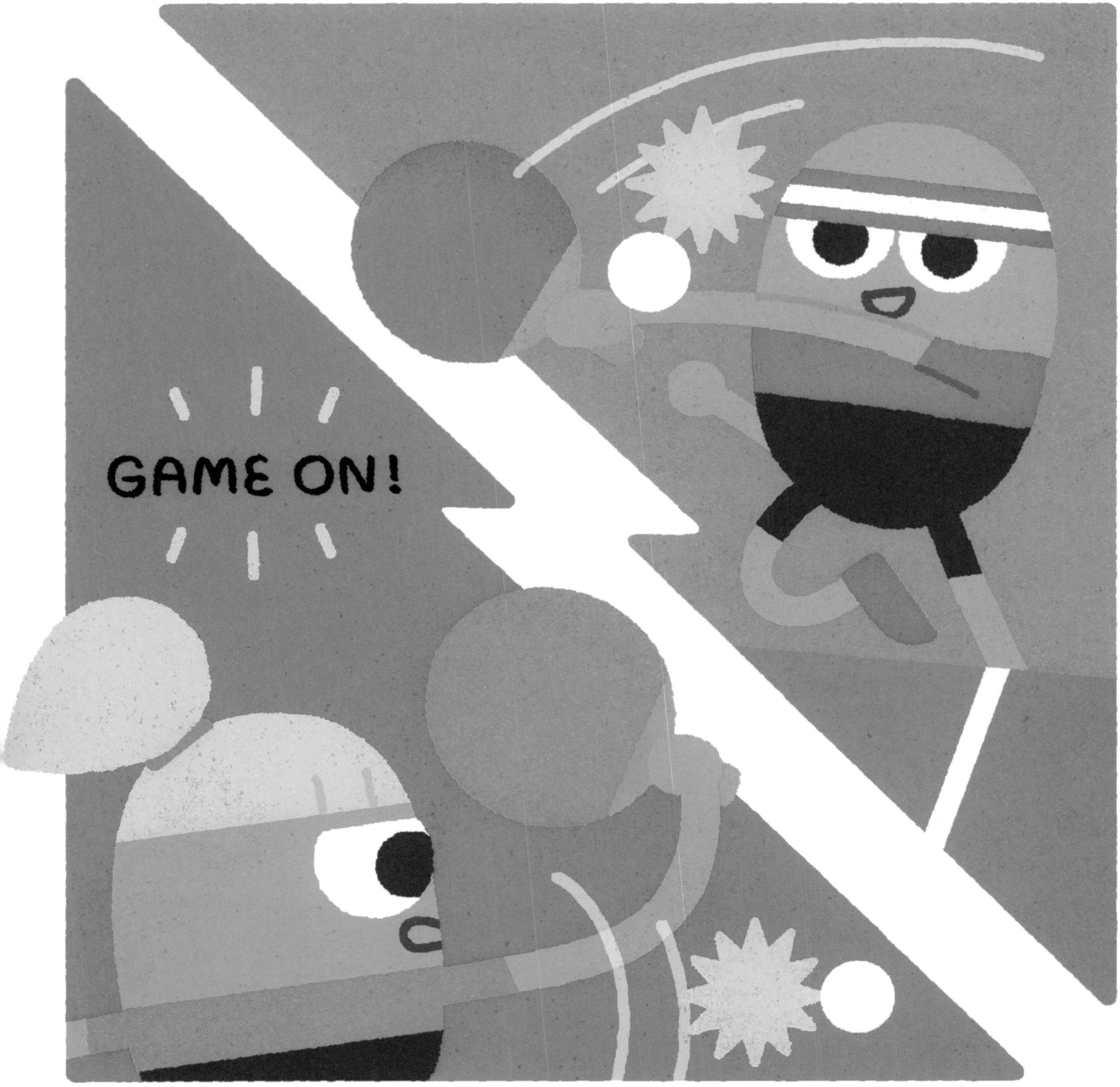
GAME ON!

Ping knew exactly
which move to do...

their famous

MIGHTY
BURNING PADDLE
SHOT!

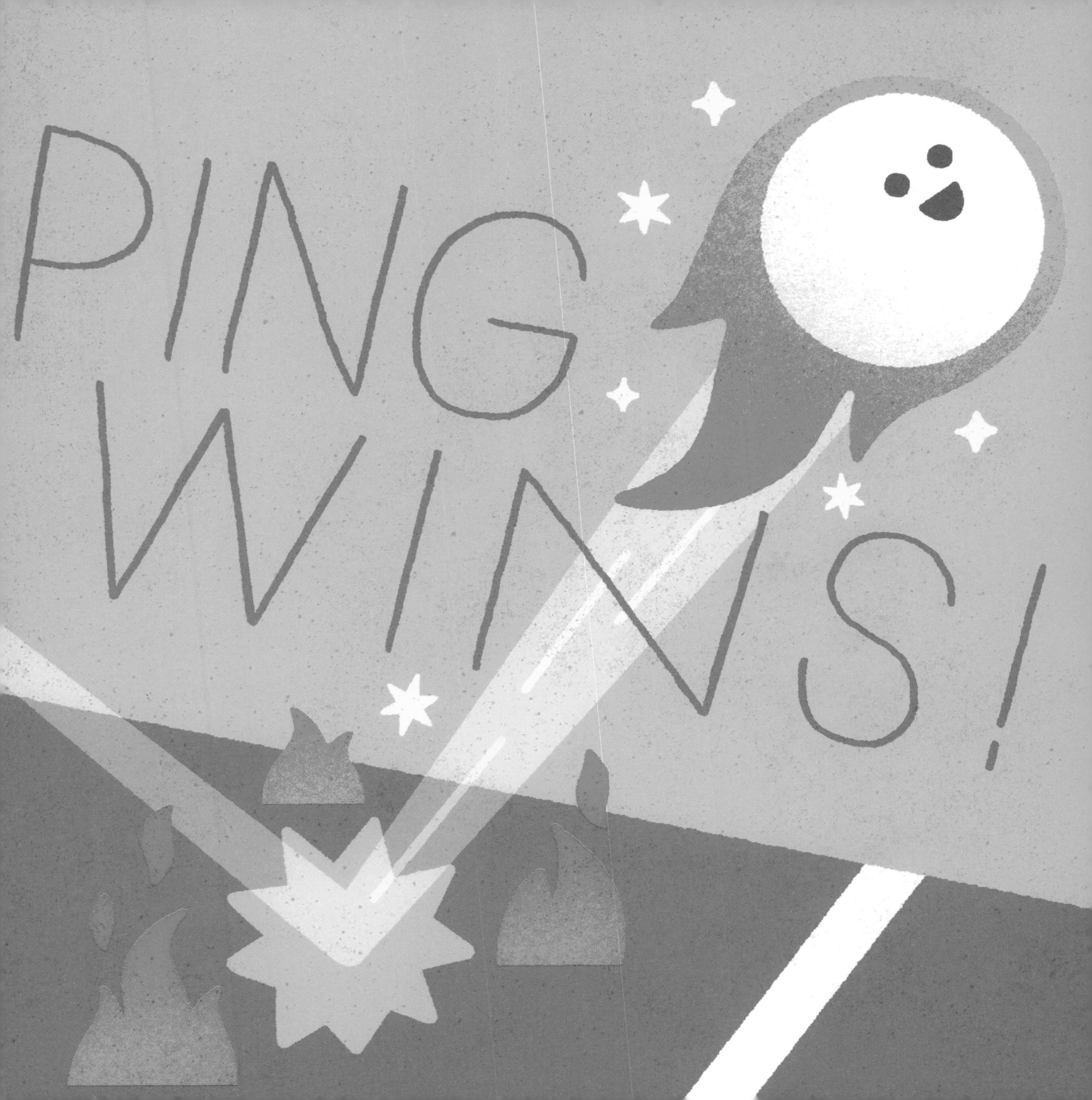
PING WINS!

There had never been a happier edamame bean in the world...

...but there had also never been
a sadder edamame bean in the world.

"Come on, Pong. Don't be sad. Just look at the crowd in the stadium! It's been a great game."

"Can you beat me in space?"

Ping and Pong kept on playing for many years.

When they became old they opened
a table tennis academy, where they taught young
edamame beans their most valuable lesson...

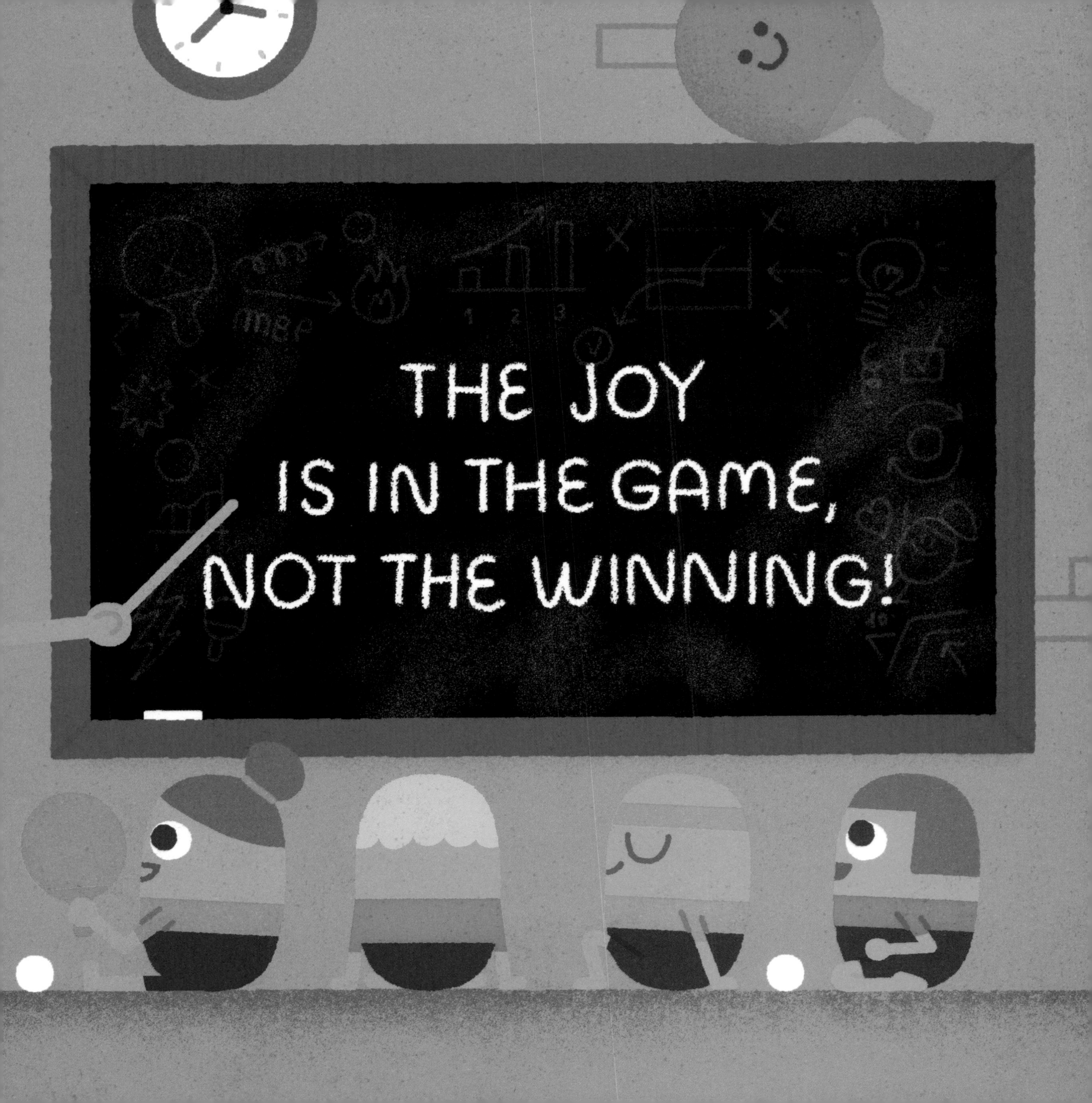
THE JOY
IS IN THE GAME,
NOT THE WINNING!